I0570544

Swan Bay Jim

An award winning short story
by Gary B. Giberson

Illustrations by Kathy Anne English

SOUTH JERSEY CULTURE & HISTORY CENTER
2017

Published 2017 by the South Jersey Culture & History Center at Stockton University.

101 Vera King Farris Drive, Galloway, NJ, 08205.

Title: Swan Bay Jim.

Author: Gary B. Giberson.

Editing, design and layout: Taylor Cills and Sarah Galzerano.

Text Copyright held by Gary B. Giberson and
South Jersey Culture & History Center.
Image Copyright held by Kathy Anne English.

ISBN: 978-0-9976699-4-7

South Jersey Culture & History Center

Foreword

Praise God!

This story is dedicated to my family and to my Grand-father, Alonzo, who taught me many things. Among those things were how to tell a story, how to manage in the Pines, and how to live life along the river. My teacher, Stephen Dunn, taught me how to put it down in writing.

I further dedicate this story to all of the people who live in the Pines and to those who will follow them.

I would also like to thank Tom Kinsella of Stockton University and his dedicated interns for the motivation and encouragement that was given to me in the publishing of the two stories in this volume.

Mayor Gary Giberson
Port Republic, New Jersey

A crow calls in the distance. The morning sun has not yet broken over the horizon, and yet the night is over. The last flake of a winter snow storm drifts to the forest floor. The gray squirrels, which live in the hollow maples that surround McCullum's Island cedar swamp, scurry about, rooting the snow for sugar gum pods full of sweet nut-like seeds. The great white-tailed deer, who is notoriously called Swan Bay Jim by the locals, is drinking from a spring. He is tired from an encounter with a younger buck. His muzzle is gray, his eyelashes pure white. A field mouse, that wishes to share the pool of water, is snorted away by the great deer.

The cedar kindling crackles in the sandstone fireplace that spans the entire north wall of Laura and Alonzo's farm house. The smell of burning cedar makes its way up the narrow stairway, which leads to the second-story room where Alonzo lies half asleep, half awake, pondering his day's chores, his aging, and his smokehouse, void of fish, eels, geese and venison.

Laura has been up and around for over an hour getting the house warm on this particular early February morning. Alonzo lifts his bulky frame, leans on one arm as the other parts the gingham drapes to reveal the sprawl of the farm yard below.

"Oh my, snow again," he grumbles.

"Lon, are you up yet?" asks Laura, as she places a pair of small oaks onto the fire.

"Well, my mind is up, but my old body is still in bed," he hollers down.

"It's too cold up there. Git down here you old fool," she insists.

The air that fills the room chills Alonzo's bare feet as they hit the wide pine floorboards. The thick quilted coverlet falls

5

Kathy Anne English

to the floor as Alonzo scratches his full belly and re-buttons the top of his flannel long johns, tight to his neck.

Alonzo yawns, he looks across the room into the gilded mirror that sits upon his shaving stand. A thin layer of ice covers the wash bowl beneath it.

He stares at his image, noting with some sadness his thinning white hair, the wrinkles on his brow, and the double chin that lies sagging under his partially-toothed mouth. He looks at his crooked fingers and moves them stiffly to and fro. He turns his hand over and notices the growing liver spots that now almost cover them. Eighty-one years have been hard on this old man, he thinks.

Alonzo reaches for his wool shirt and heavy corduroy pants that rest close by on the back of his favorite oak rocker. He dresses and makes his way down the stairs, adjusting his wide green suspenders as he bumps from side to side.

"Save them two day old eggs fer sumpin' else," he warns Laura. "I'll fetch us a couple warm ones from the coop." He pulls on his cut-off Gold Seal hip boots, ties his hand-crocheted scarf around his neck, and with Laura's help, pulls on his heavy Woolrich Mackinaw.

"You'll catch yer death fer a couple of fresh eggs, you old fool," she scorns. Alonzo pinches her cheek and makes his way to the door.

"Fry us up some sweet taters," he requests, as he adjusts the brim of his brown corduroy hat.

"Pull down them ear flaps," Laura shouts at him as he goes out the door.

The new fallen snow is five inches deep. It is moist and heavy, as most snows are from the northeast, he thinks. But the wind that bites at his face is coming from the west now. It'll be a cold day, he thinks.

He lifts his head to hear his neighbor's Jersey heifer bawling for her early milking a half mile down the road. A closer knocking sound causes Alonzo to stop and turn around. It is coming from the dog house that stands close to the woodshed.

His prize black and tan Walker coonhound is standing up in his tight surroundings, his tail is hitting the sides. Only his nose sticks out of the cramped quarters, pushing aside the burlap curtain door.

"Too cold fer ya this mornin'?" Alonzo asks.

He walks behind the woodshed to gather an armful of salt hay to warm old Jack's ears, then stiffly gets up and goes off in the direction of the hen coop.

Alonzo fumbles through the nest boxes, lifting his hens to see if they have done their part to yield a pair of warm fresh eggs for their breakfast.

"At last," he says to one of his Rhode Island Reds.

He carefully places the eggs into his cap, and with great caution, puts his cap back on.

From the hen coop he makes his way to the smokehouse. Alonzo walks slowly toward it, as he makes up his mind whether to have ham or bacon. He pulls a butcher knife from one of the studs that is loaded with the smell of hickory smoke. It is too dull to cut the bacon, he decides.

A short walk in the opposite direction from the hen coop stands Alonzo's great barn, its stalls now void of livestock. Only cobwebs fill their emptiness. The harnesses that hang nearby are dry and cracking.

Alonzo breaks away at the ice that has locked up his whetstone grinding wheel. He begins to turn the heavy stone wheel. The sparks flying from the smokehouse knife mesmerize his thoughts as the knife becomes sharp. He looks around the barn. His rotting cotton gill nets hang over his head, and the hayloft is packed with his rusting muskrat traps.

Fish in the summer, muskrats in the winter, how damn lucky I've been, he thinks, to live on this place next to the Mullica River, where my father's father trapped and fished. They had cut the cedars that had built all them great ships, he thinks. He looks down at the earthen floor of his barn. Rich Jersey soil, look how dark it is. I remember the corn, and God bless them pole limas.

He turns the knife over and quenches the glowing edge in the water trough below the wheel. He runs his finger across the blade, a little dull on the point, he thinks. He begins to turn the wheel again. The sparks drift Alonzo back into his memories. The tools hanging around him look dull and rusty. Their wood handles are warped and split with dryness.

"My whole damn life is rustin', crackin', splitin' and shrivelin' up," he says aloud, as if the wheel could hear him. His eyes become dampened to the point where he has to blink them clear. The barn cat who has joined him begins to walk around his legs and rub against them. Its loud purring cannot be heard above the grinding sound of the knife against the wheel, but somehow the cat's presence makes him feel better.

Alonzo looks to the rafters. He takes in a deep breath. Nailed five to a side on one pair of rafters are ten sets of antlers from the white-tailed deer he had successfully hunted. The antlers bring thoughts of better times to his mind.

"Some men hunt all their lives an' never git one, but I got ten of 'em," he tells the cat. Good number, ten, he thinks. I got ten fingers, I got ten toes, I got me ten deer. He looks at the rafters again. The space above the antler racks, close to where the rafters meet at the ridge, is empty, as if waiting for something to be placed there.

The knife is totally sharp now. Alonzo's thoughts are back on the bacon. The cat does not follow him to the smokehouse, the snow is too deep for its warm paws.

"I'll fetch you some breakfast," he says to the cat. Alonzo cuts three inches of bacon from the slab and a small portion for his friend the cat, and another for old Jack. He replaces the sharp knife into the smokehouse stud and returns to the barn. As he swings the barn door open, the low winter sun behind him enters the darkened barn. The cat smells the hickory bacon and jumps up close to the door, but Alonzo's attention is drawn to the ridge — to the empty space. The sun over his shoulder is like a spotlight shining directly on it.

"Swan Bay Jim," he murmers to the feeding cat. "I saved that spot fer his antlers." Images race through his thoughts as he remembers the great deer that has eluded him all his life.

"No one could ever git him."

The cat pays no attention to Alonzo's mutterings. The bacon has his entire attention.

Alonzo looks about the cobwebs. He looks at the crackling harnesses, the rusting tools, his nets that will fish no more, his traps that will not be set again.

"The wind is right," he says as he closes the door, watching the lit space disappear at the ridge.

He makes his way back to the house. His stride gets bouncy as a new desire grows inside him. He tosses Jack his breakfast.

Once in the house, Alonzo nearly drops the eggs as he removes his cap. He places them on the table with the three inches of bacon. His sweet potatoes are sizzling on the cast iron skillet behind him.

"Here ye are woman, cook 'em up in a hurry, cause I got somewheres to go this mornin'."

Kathy Anne English

"Where you gotta go this mornin'?"

"I gotta git him today. The wind is right!"

"Who you gotta git?" Laura asks as she slices the bacon.

"Swan Bay Jim, that's who."

"You old fool!"

"The wind is right. He'll be a layin' in McCullum's Island swamp this mornin'. I know, damn it, I know. The snow is just right, and with this west wind, I'll walk right up on him."

"You ain't bin a huntin' fer years. What has come over you? You can't go off a huntin'. That deer has out-foxed you all yer life. Why, no mortal has been able to git'im, no dog can stay onto his track."

"Have some faith. Have some faith," Alonzo answers.

Laura just mutters back, "You old fool, sit down an' eat."

"I'll be a needin' an extra pair of socks. Will you fetch me down a pair?" Alonzo asks, as he gulps down his unchewed food.

"You should be a thinkin' on all them chores you been lettin' slide by."

"Please, hon, I'll drink up a full quart of water tonight. Tomorrow mornin' we'll just stay under them quilts an' . . . ."

"You old fool," Laura says with a smile, as she goes off to get his socks.

"Let me wrap you up some fresh warm biscuits," Laura offers.

"No, thanks, I'll be home befer lunch. This here west wind got quite a bite on to it." He re-buttons his Woolrich coat.

Alonzo walks to the sandstone wall and takes down his ten-gauge Parker shotgun. He blows off the dust and wipes it down with a tea towel that hangs nearby. He fills his coat pocket with a handful of double "O" buckshot shells.

"Don't ferget yer mittens." Laura rubs his shoulders, as if to wish him good luck. "Be careful."

Old Jack sees Alonzo with his Parker in hand and begins to bark and bay. The black and tan pulls at his chain and drags his dog house toward Alonzo. The snow, which builds up in front of it, brings the dog to a sudden stop.

"Not today, Ol' Jack. The wind is wrong fer ya, but not fer me. I'll put it onto 'im today fer sure," he tells the dog. The dog stops barking when Alonzo crosses the field and enters the thick laurel bushes at the edge of the woods road that leads to McCullum's Island swamp. Alonzo fumbles for his buckshot, loads his Parker, and pulls the hammers to half-cock.

He'll be a layin' on a clump of sphagnum moss near a cedar spring, thinks Alonzo. That spring water is warmer than the air this mornin'.

His shotgun becomes heavy and he switches it often from shoulder to shoulder. He makes his way through the woods. He remembers how his father had taught him to stalk a white-tailed deer. Move slow into the wind. Don't break a dead branch or step on dry twigs. Move ahead three steps, then wait, move ahead two steps, wait, look around, move four more. He stalks up to the "Old Place" where his grandfather had once had a home in the woods.

It is here that he comes across the track of the great deer, Swan Bay Jim. It is easy to recognize. His right front hoof print tells the story of their first meeting.

Alonzo had found the deer, a mere fawn, caught in his gill net one morning eighteen years ago, at the mouth of Big Creek. He saved him from drowning, but could not repair the damage done to the young buck's hoof by the thin mesh of the net. It never did completely mend.

He removes his mittens and drops to his knee. He measures the distance between the deer's prints in the snow,

of his hind and front leg, by spreading his little finger and thumb to their limits, and walking them across the snow like an inch worm.

He is slowing down, thinks Alonzo, for he had measured this stride many times before. He looks off in the direction of the tracks.

He's a headin' right fer the swamp, Alonzo thinks. Old Jim had never done that before. He'd always wander around, never head fer it. You're a gittin' a might careless in your old age, Alonzo thinks of the deer.

Alonzo thinks of the last time he came upon the deer's track with a gun in hand. He remembers how his stalk was ruined by moving too quickly. He is aware that the deer has stopped frequently this time, as if to rest.

He presses on with skill and anticipation, his breathing quickens, his heart pounds harder. A few hundred feet pass and Alonzo comes upon fresh droppings left by Old Jim. Again, he removes his mittens to see if there is any warmth left in the round pellets that lie on the snow. There is, and also a trace of blood. Further on he comes to an area of snow that reveals that the great deer had fallen.

"He's a hurtin'," Alonzo says aloud, covering his mouth as the words escape. He can see where the deer's nose has struck the snow, and the large antlers have left their mark.

Alonzo again looks in the direction of the track. Before him is the stand of maples and gum trees that surround the cedar swamp.

As the sun rises behind him, he knows that the wind will pick up, and that the deer, blinded by the sun, will not be able to see him as he comes nearer.

There he was — just as Alonzo had thought. Old Swan Bay Jim, lying on a clump of sphagnum moss next to a cedar spring. The mist in the swamp proves Alonzo's theory, that the air was colder than the water that rose from the ground.

Alonzo bites off the mitten from his right hand with his teeth. He slowly and deliberately raises his Parker to his shoulder. He pulls the hammers to full-cock. His finger freezes on the lead trigger.

The deer becomes aware of Alonzo's presence and jumps to his feet with a loud snort. It is the first time anything has been able to get this close to the deer without him sensing or knowing it.

The great deer takes in a lung full of air. He is left with no way out of his predicament. Old Jim paws the snow and moss that cover his front hoofs. He lowers his great neck, points his antlers at Alonzo and charges.

Alonzo is terrified and cannot move. His mind tells him to pull the trigger, but like this morning in bed, his body and fingers will not wake up.

The deer leaps at him, but the deer's judgment has failed him too.

Swan Bay Jim falls dead in the snow a few feet in front of Alonzo. The vapor through his nostrils let out the last signal of life. Alonzo can only shake for a moment. He looks at Old Jim in disbelief. His knees become weak. His heart pounds. He gasps for more air to fill his burning lungs.

The stillness is broken by Alonzo's scream: "OH NO why my God why? . . . . You poor old bastard."

A warm tear makes its way down Alonzo's cold cheek. He raises the Parker to his shoulder, aims at the cedar tops, and fires off both barrels at the same time.

The kick from the gun hurts his shoulder. The deafening sound echoes from the cedars around him. It can be heard as it reaches the river banks off to his right, and again from the area of his farm in back of him.

Kathy Anne English

Nervous crows in the distance call out the signal of a hunter's presence.

Alonzo kneels . . . .

Kathy Anne English

www.ingramcontent.com/pod-product-compliance
Lightning Source LLC
Chambersburg PA
CBHW050917120626
46552CB00004B/1626

* 9 7 8 0 9 9 7 6 6 9 9 4 7 *

Gasoline Seventeen Cents a Gallon; Moonshine a Dollar a Quart

A short story by Gary B. Giberson

South Jersey Culture & History Center
2017

Published 2017 by the South Jersey Culture & History Center at Stockton University.

101 Vera King Farris Drive, Galloway, NJ, 08205.

Title: Gasoline Seventeen Cents a Gallon; Moonshine a Dollar a Quart.

Author: Gary B. Giberson.

Editing, design and layout: Taylor Cills and Sarah Galzerano.

Copyright held by Gary B. Giberson and South Jersey Culture & History Center.

ISBN: 978-0-9976699-4-7

South Jersey Culture & History Center

Gasoline Seventeen Cents a Gallon; Moonshine a Dollar a Quart

"Are you really the mayor?" asked young Henry as he looked into the deep blue eyes of his favorite Grandfather.

"Yep, still am, and I ran the town gas station!" Pop Pop Gary replied.

It was a typical Sunday, and the Giberson Family had all come together at Gary and Niki's farm for their family dinner after church. All the dishes were cleared, and the children followed Pop Pop into their family room where four large sofas circled a crackling fire in the large fire place. The older children, Jesse, Sadie, Judah, Peter and Micah, pulled pillows off of the sofas and threw them at Pop Pop's feet. The two lucky youngest got a favorite knee spot.

"Is everybody ready?" he asked. "Are you sure you don't want to watch some TV?"

"No! No! No!" came a quick reply. "We want to hear you tell a story."

"OK," Pop Pop replied, "but first I have to tell you this story takes place during the Great Depression of the late 1920s to the early 1930s."

"What does that mean?" asked Molly, the left-knee-sitter.

Pop Pop went on, "It just means that these were hard times to live in, and jobs and a way to earn money were few and far between. Some folks were so desperate they broke the law by making illegal whiskey called moonshine. It was usually made by the light of the moon, in the woods or someplace where these moonshiners could hide their activities from the police

3

and government people who were sworn, by law, to put them out of business."

Pop Pop continued, trying to set the story he was about to tell so the youngsters could understand. "During the Great Depression, people could not make, sell, distribute or even drink alcoholic beverages, beer, whiskey and stuff like that, during these times known as Prohibition. The government made a very big federal amendment law to our constitution which was the main law of the land."

"OK, OK," little Sadie and Henry butted in in unison as they usually did. "Let's hear this story!"

"You bet!" said Pop Pop as he could see his young audience turning and twitching.

"Now then . . .

Crows call in the distance breaking the stillness in the air. Seems one day some men from the town of Unionville in Southern New Jersey, located on the historic Mullica River, were a sitten' around the country gas station at the corner of Clark's Landing Road and Mill Street. The smell of stale tobacco juice spit, gasoline, and dirty sludge oil drifts through one's nostrils. Waxed glue flypaper hangs from the ceiling of the cluttered station office, not yet completely full of those pesky germ-carrying, winged buggers known as pine flies. The walls are full of period advertising and a girly calendar shows the year 1931. Bills to be collected are jammed behind some loose wiring that has seen better days. A wall telephone hangs, with a hand cranking device used to "ring up an operator," and a pendulum clock remains still as if time has stopped.

A sixteen-tube cathedral radio cabinet — so called as it resembles the front of a house of God — sits on the desk of the station. Static and interference from the nearby Tuckerton wireless

station, which is broadcasting in Morse code to radio stations in Europe, breaks the silence in the gas station office room.

Outside sits the owner, who is pressing the men gathered at the usual meeting place for some good old-man gossip. In this area between the front office and the gas pump island sits the glass-cock coke box full of hand chopped ice cool'en down some Nehi and Coca-Cola. Bottle caps are scattered around the area as the men are interested in hear'en the latest news.

"Here comes that cheap tightwad from Smithville in that new shiny little American Austin Bantam car! (A car named after a banty rooster, adds Pop Pop.) He would drive fer miles to save a penny on gas!" remarks a wittl'n guy with one-suspender overalls that hadn't seen the inside of a washtub in months.

"Yea, he'll try to bum a soda-pop or sumpt'em!" remarks the fellow two seats down.

As the 1931 Bantam pulls up to the pump, another news-spreader quickly suggests, "Let's ignore the bugger and his little car an' not give'em the time of day."

"Morn'en boys," the tightwad exclaims as he quickly shuts down his small car to save gas. No one lifts his head or pays any attention to this fellow who has interrupted their privacy.

"Did you fellows hear 'bout them Weavers up there on Clarks Land'en Road? They all got drunk on their shine and shot up their own barn last night!"

All of a sudden heads lift, and the boys who are hungry for happen news take a total interest in old tightwad's tale.

"Wind being out of the Nor-west last night, I didn't hear anything at'tall from them boys out there," remarks the gentleman who suggested they ignore the tightwad. All of a sudden he wants to prod tightwad for some more news about this here happen'en. "Go on, Go on!" he begs.

"Well the way I heared it from their neighbors, the Wallenbacks, seems they had some visitors from that far off Chicago land who have been running their shine down the Mullica River and over to Brigantine and Atlantic City regular. Got to sampling some of old Weaver's good stuff and put on a show with the use of them there 'tommy guns' they all carry. Seems they were try'en to spell their names with bullet holes on the barn walls!"

"GO ON, GO ON," the group insists.

Old tightwad continues, "Yep they shot up the whole side of that there barn, and when I drove past there this morning, them Weavers, they were all out there whittlen' down cedar shingles to plug most them holes, I spect they'll be up here soon to buy more shingles off Lon Giberson's cedar sawmill."

All the folks in the area were aware of the special trade of the Weaver family but were very close lipped about mentioning it in front of any stranger in fear that that there stranger just might be "a revenuer."

"Yep, that there Weaver family sure do hang out with some pretty scary folks!" says old tightwad. The men begin to

whisper and nod, in fear of letting this news get back to the Weavers, as they might be just a bit dangerous.

Mayor Gary emerges from the front of the garage office. He had gone back to answer his phone. Now he starts toward his old Mae West gas pump, named after buxom Mae West, the motion picture queen: big top, narrow waist, and a well-rounded bottom.

"How much gas you want today? And should I check your oil or maybe give the wind-up key a turn or two that drives this little baby down the road?" he asks.

Old tightwad replies, "Just seventeen cents worth, or one gallon — whichever she will hold. And no, my oil is ok!"

Mayor Gary lifts the hood of the Austin to get to the small gas tank located just above its very small four-cylinder motor — about the size of a Singer sewing machine. Mayor Gary winks toward the boys who were all a'smiling at the cheap order of this particular sale. "Sure glad more people don't pull in here fer seventeen cents worth of gas. I'd be out of business pretty quick," states the Mayor.

All the boys laugh and slap one another on the back. Old tightwad fumbles through his pocket and pulls out money in change to pay for his purchase. As the Mayor hangs up the Mae West hose and nozzle, tightwad hands him the money.

"You're two cents shy," the Mayor remarks.

Old tightwad turns his back to all and carefully fumbles through his loose change for two more pennies. He turns, complaining about the price of gas these days, "You'd think them oil people would know there's a depression on, an' lower the prices of this here stuff so we could afford more!"

The men all laugh and snicker. This upsets old tightwad even more.

"I had to drive all the way over here 'cause old Al Ramsey, he gets nineteen cents a gallon fer his.

The boys are really almost laugh'en at him now, and one remarks, "Maybe you should ask Mr. Weaver fer a job still-stok'en. After all he gets one dollar a quart fer shine!"

"Guess none of you here guys would offer me a soda?" asks old tightwad.

Almost in unison they all answer, "Guess not!"

Old tightwad quickly jumps in his tiny car, slams the door shut, rolls down the door window and hollers as he drives off, "I'm a gonna tell them Weaver boys you've all been a'talking about all their activities and their house guests last night!"

The men all jump to their feet and all look to the ground for something to fling at the small shiny black car, which now is covered with a cloud of dust, never in its life driven that fast. The men all look at one another as if they had swallowed glass. One remarks, "You don't think old tightwad was a kidd'en us do you?"

Mayor Gary sees an opportunity to rub in some conviction, "Next time you all might want to buy him a soda. God knows times are tough!"

Mayor Gary yawns and pulls up his suspenders, giving them a snap as if to help get him awake and ready for another unique day at his garage. He looks forward to the tasks at hand: a radiator to re-solder for Joe Champion, a fan belt to install on Ann Pierce's Model T Ford — "If she drove the speed limits, she would stop throw'en fan belts," he thought — then the big job of re-grinding the valves on Francis Huntley's Dodge pick-up truck.

As usual, breakfast is interrupted by someone need'en gas before open'en time. This car is an out-of-state large black Cadillac limo-type, a sixteen-cylinder model with a chauffeur who sits in the open while his boss sits in pure luxury in the rear part of this long wheelbase model. It looks like it could haul an army.

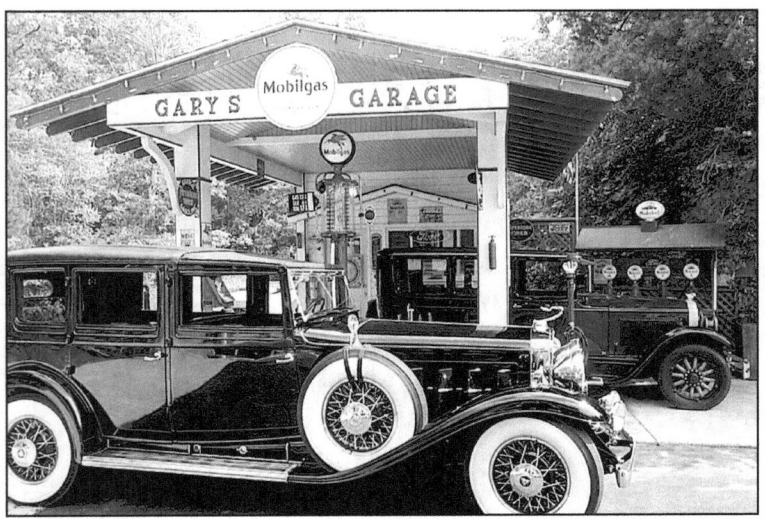

"What can I get for you this early morn'en?" asks the Mayor. As he approaches the large car, he sees that two tough-looking, large men sit in the front, and it looks like two or three huskier, stout men are in the rear.

"Fill'er up, and check the oil," is the quick reply as the Mayor quickly notices them trying to conceal something that looks like a pistol.

The memory of yesterday's tightwad story suddenly enters the Mayor's thoughts as he nervously starts to hand-pump the gasoline out of the ground and into the 10-gallon visual glass container on top of his Mae West pump. "Glad you boys got me out here early. Them troopers with them noisy Harley cycles will be here 'bout this here time, and they hate a'wait'en on me and my breakfast."

"Never mind the oil!" someone shouts from the rear of the big black car. "We're running late this morning. We have to run with the tide, remember."

"That's it," the Mayor thinks. "For sure, these here fellows are rum runners on their way to the still and then down

Clarks Landing, where I bet their white lightn'en whiskey will be loaded."

He quickly fills the big black car's tank and nervously spills almost half a gallon. "That will be one dollar and seventy cents," the Mayor exclaims as he walks toward the driver.

Quickly a very large arm emerges out the back window, and in its hand is a crisp new ten-dollar bill. "Keep the change!" is the reply to the Mayor's request.

As the rear window quickly rolls up, the large motor starts and purrs like a tiger as it quickly disappears around the bend in the road that leads to Clarks Landing.

"It sure is good being the Mayor," he thinks. "Taught me to think quick when put in a sticky corner and always to say the right thing. Now where did I leave my soldering iron? And I forgot what time I told Joe Champion his radiator would be fixed . . . Well this day is off to a good start."

The Mayor removes the ten spot given him and snaps it twice before ringing up one dollar and seventy cents, placing it under the cash register bill separator with a great big grin. "Them boys in Cadillac, Michigan, sure do know how to put an automobile together," he exclaims aloud as if someone could hear.

"Never had so darn many interruptions in one day," Mayor Gary tells Francis Huntley from his wall phone. "I'll stay on it after supper, Francis, and you can have her back tomorrow morn'en fer sure."

There's nothing poor Francis can do but go with the plan, as his engine is all apart on Mayor Gary's garage floor and work bench. As usual, supper is right on time, and the Mayor's wife, Niki, has made up a plate for him to eat in the garage. "Boy, I love them smoked pork chops with potato salad, succotash, and homemade applesauce," he tells Niki.

His wife sits down with him and prepares herself to watch the garage's island in case a car drives up, which almost always happens before the Mayor can finish his supper. She promises him a hot cup of coffee, and goes back to the house, soon to return with the coffee pot full of newly perked coffee.

"I'll put it on the hot plate so as to keep it warm as you need it." She wipes his greasy cheek off with the corner of her apron and kisses it softly.

The night seems long as that old Dodge gets her valves reground. "A new head gasket and tune the carburetor a bit and she'll run like a kitten," he thinks. As he closes the hood down and wipes his hands as clean as the dirty rag he uses will allow, he pulls the light off in the garage. He enters the station office and writes out Francis Huntley's bill. "Francis and Linda have some great chickens. Maybe I'll mention a barter trade with 'em," he thinks.

After putting all the gas station's island items away, Mayor Gary closes down the station, locks up the front door, and chains down the Coke icebox and its contents.

"Long day," he thinks as he pushes hard at his back with both hands to take away some creep'en pains.

"Tomorrow it's change the points in Mike Turner's Fordson tractor and change its oil. Gosh, I hate to drive that tractor that cuts up my driveway with them steel-cheated wheels."

After a quick look around for left-out tools, the Mayor pulls his pocket watch from his greasy coverall trousers to check the hour. "Good Lord, it's after midnight!" he exclaims out loud as if there was someone to hear his complaint.

Just as he starts to leave, he hears a large — a very large truck a'roaring down the road coming from Clarks Landing. They're driving the truck with no lights on, trusting the clouds won't cover the moon's light as it shines through the trees. He steps back from the road till the speeding truck passes. The Mayor can

see the outline of a large brown waxed canvas tarp covering the truck's load in the back from view. He thinks to himself, "I sure know what them there boys are up to at this hour. Them there rum runners. Why are they a go'en down Sooy's Landing Road?"

Curiosity gets the best of him. Niki's black coffee had gotten stronger as the night of long labor has drawn on, and he is wide awake, not too tired to go on a sneak watch. He grabs his old Columbia bicycle and pedals as fast as he can down Sooy's Landing. At the end of the tree line he parks his bike behind a clump of swamp maples and red cedars, crouches low, and takes off on foot where the meadows and road meet. At the very end of the road is the landing where Sooy's Creek meanders in from Swan Bay, the widest part of the Mullica River.

The rum runners are being very careful not to make any noise, downloading them wooden crates full of one-dollar-a-quart moonshine whiskey. There is a slight breeze, and the tall cattail reeds that surround the landing are gently swaying, which allows cover for the Mayor to slip up close to the busy men. There are two men from the truck and two men in the sea skiff that is tied up to a makeshift docking area. The Mayor recognizes the voices of the men in the boat as old Captain John Fish from Absecon and his sidekick, one of them Rinaldo brothers from Pleasantville. They had both whittled cedar carvings on many occasions at his garage.

The Mayor makes himself comfortable and watches as each case is carefully stored aboard the sea skiff. "Got to be at least forty quarts in each case," Mayor Gary thinks, and he begins to count the cases as they finish unloading.

"Two rows ten crates long, five high . . . That's one hundred cases with forty quarts at one dollar a quart." He pauses as he tries to multiply in his mind. "Wow, those guys have four thousand dollars' worth of illegal booze on that little skiff. That's enough to buy ten new Model A Fords."

The rum runners all stay perfectly still for a good two minutes, with their hands cupped close to their ears, trying to hear if there is any other activity on the river up near Clarks Landing where they usually off-load their moonshine. When assured by pure silence, one motion from Captain Fish and the boat engine starts. The skiff pulls away slowly as the truck driver and his partner head for their truck. The men begin to scrape the mud off the license plates on their truck that were covered so no one could report the registered number of the truck used during their illegal activities. After the large canvas tarp is folded and loaded, they turn around and carefully and slowly go on their way. The Mayor quickly scratches the freshly revealed plate number into the gravel road with a broken-off cattail reed stem.

The Mayor waits until he can no longer hear the skiff's powerful Ford V-8 sixty motor and then runs back to his bike, toward his garage and home.

As he pedals he thinks to himself, "I guess I'm not the only one who had to work late tonight."

It's the middle of the week just about two days after the Mayor's extra nighttime work and spy'en opportunity. The Mayor fixes a flat tire and charges a battery for his close friend Brian Artman, who is a very talented artist and a maker of stool ducks — often called decoys.

Brian is a special friend because he is always offering to help anybody that needs him. He would drive older folks anywhere they wanted to go, and for some reason he loves to push that old rusty lawn mower of his. He would mow folk's lawns just for a cold drink of lemonade and never take a nickel.

Brian is such a good friend, Mayor Gary knows he can trust him. He shares his spying adventure, telling the story over in great picture tell'en fashion.

Brian is always smiling. Sometimes you wondered what he was think'en about. This day Brian's face lights up, and his eyeballs look like golf balls as the Mayor's story and experience are revealed.

"What are you gonna do about that, Mayor?" he asks.

The Mayor thinks for some while before he answers his friend. "Well, good friend, I sure as heck should do something. I am the Mayor. I'm personally responsible for the public safety of the folks in this here town of Unionville."

Brian asks again, this time standing in front of the Mayor. Pulling his hands off the tire tube he says, "OK, Mayor Gary. How can I help you do something?"

"Don't worry Brian. It's already in the troopers' hands," he tells him confidentially.

The Mayor continues, "Be quiet now, let me fix this here patch before the glue dries." The two friends insert the repaired tube into a well-worn tire and refit the wheel onto Brian's Chevy. The Mayor pulls the charger cables off the battery and sets it beneath the floorboards of Brian's car.

Brian gives the Mayor ten cents for the patch and another twenty-five for the charge.

Mayor Gary tells Brian, "Only one more charge left in that battery. Want me to order you in a new one at my cost?"

"Sure, Mayor Gary. I'm a work'en on a big commission job painting a sign for some farmer who has to sell his farm. He wants me to show his children a'crying holding onto their Mom's apron. It's an 'involved paint,'" Brian explains, as he putt-putts off.

The Mayor turns around to see a total stranger all dressed up like he's off to Sunday church.

"Yes sir, what can old Mayor Gary do fer you?" he asks.

The stranger stares into the Mayor's eyes as he goes to his right rear pocket to remove his wallet. Flicking it open he shows him his silver badge, stating loudly, "Agent Donald Dunbar of the Federal Government!"

Mayor Gary stares into Agent Donald's eyes as he reaches for his own wallet. "Mayor Gary Giberson, Mayor of the town of Unionville," as he flips open his wallet to reveal a gold badge twice the size of the agent's.

The surprised agent steps back, and his tone suddenly changes. Both men are in shock at what happens next. Up pulls a Harley-Davidson State Police motorcycle. The rider is dressed in his hightop black boots, with blue-gray rid'en britches with gold stripes. His cap visor is covered with gold braid, and his matching jacket sports the triangle badge standing on its point. The sleeves of his jacket are sporting many gold bars depicting his many years of service. His aviator glasses and high wrist black leather gloves complete his magnificent appearance.

It's Mayor Gary's friend and duck-hunting partner, State Police Captain Smith from the District A Barracks in Hammonton. He has the three Weaver brothers in handcuffs,

15

making them walk in front of his motorcycle with a single rope around all their necks. They're crusty and all smell of sour mash, fermenting corn and coal oil.

"I want to thank you, Mayor, and the folks here in Unionville for all your help in this case. We didn't get the boat men, but got three in Brigantine, five in Atlantic City, and a couple of guys in a big black Cadillac from out of state, who confessed to their wrong doings after we found their names shot into the Weaver's barn. And, by the way, hello, Agent Dunbar."

The G-man is silent, feeling embarrassed that he had nothing to do with the conclusion of the case that he was sent to solve. One of the Weaver Boys spits tobacco juice on his shiny brown shoes. He makes a quick exit, jumps into his Nash coupe and quickly drives off.

The Mayor thinks, "Nash never did make a good car."

Two black and white Ford trooper patrol cars pull up, and after chaining up their feet and legs they load them Weaver boys in.

As everyone leaves but Captain Smith, he asks Mayor Gary to go up to the Weaver farm with him in his tow truck and trailer and bring out the dismantled still and all the other evidence that they had found.

When the Mayor has it all in tow with his shiny new tow truck with trailer, he makes a complete loop all over Unionville, then drives to the Hammonton State Police impoundment yard, with all the goods in hand.

"Them Weaver boys will be out on bail in a week or two and find another hiding place. Maybe they could make up a traveling still or something." Mayor Gary can't help thinking of the stories that would fly around Mayor Gary's Garage next Saturday.

"Yes, times were a bit hard but fun and exciting here in the woods. God seems to look out for us country folks, so always be on His side of things that someday might trouble you."

"What about tightwad?" questions Judah.

"Yeah," says Peter.

"Did you ever taste that moonshine Pop Pop?" asks Micah. Sadie just smiles.

"Pop Pop was that a true story?" asks the oldest child, Jesse

"Yep!" is his reply, "If you have a good enough imagination anything can be true."

This story is dedicated to my family and friends and to all the folks who got us through these hard times and fought two World Wars and left us with the freedoms we take for granted today.

May GOD continue to bless us . . . .